IN THE DARKNESS, EYES AND TEETH

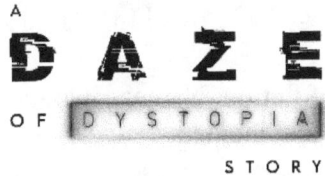

A

OF DYSTOPIA

STORY

BY FELIX I.D. DIMARO

IN THE DARKNESS, EYES AND TEETH

Written by FELIX I.D. DIMARO

Cover Artwork and Interior Artwork: Rosco Nischler
Typography: Courtney Swank
Editing: Ally Sztrimbely

Copyright © 2024 by FELIX I.D. DIMARO

ALSO BY FELIX I.D. DIMARO

How To Make A Monster: The Loveliest Shade of Red

Bug Spray: A Tale of Madness

Viral Lives: A Ghost Story

2222

The Fire on Memory Lane

The Corruption of Philip Toles

Black Bloom: A Story of Survival

Us In Pieces: Stories of Shattered Souls

Humane Sacrifice: The Story of the Aztec Killer

Daily Special: A How To Make A Monster Novella

Warning

This story contains mature content, including explicit and derogatory language, adult themes, and scenes depicting graphic violence.

Discretion is advised.

To Barbra Streisand. Thank you for the inspiration

And to Cat

"You can clone the look of a dog, but you can't clone the soul."

Barbra Streisand

"Thank God for Barbra Streisand," Madeleine Miller muttered reverently as she witnessed the miracle in front of her. If she hadn't heard about what the legendary entertainer had done with her dog, the unbelievable act unfolding before Madeleine would not be happening. Even as she witnessed it, she could barely believe it was real.

Madeleine and her husband, Douglas, were inside of a building she thought of as a facility. It was not quite a medical center, it was not quite an animal hospital, it was not quite a science laboratory. It was some fusion of the three.

Inside of an exam room, surrounding a stainless-steel table upon which was a birthing bed, the couple, along with the biotechnologist who owned the facility, stood watching a cat give birth. That in itself was no miracle (other than it being the standard miracle of life). What was so astounding about this birth was that the kitten being born was already dead.

Padmé Miller, a rare Chartreux breed, charcoal gray, shorthaired, with highlighter yellow eyes, had died two years prior. Yet Padmé Miller, with her short gray hair was right there. Reborn.

Jesus, Lazarus, John the Baptist, and now Padmé.

She was wet with afterbirth from the tawny tabby cat she had been pushed out of. But it was her, exactly as she had looked when she was a kitten. The first time. Twelve years before this day.

"There she is! She looks perfect!" Douglas exclaimed. There was as much relief as there was excitement in his voice. He had been concerned about the process from the start. But Madeleine had had faith because Barbra had led the way. And now they were here, and so was Padmé, and things were just as they were supposed to be. Except...

"What's wrong with her?" Madeleine asked, referring to the cat not the kitten. The surrogate on the table was still clearly agitated, shifting about, making soft sounds indicating struggle.

The biotech raised a finger, parted his lips, went to answer, but the surrogate made whatever he might have said unnecessary when she began to push a second kitten out of her.

To Madeleine's astonishment, the tawny cat gave birth to two other kittens following Padmé. And after all three kittens had been licked clean by their surrogate mother, Madeleine observed that they each had short gray hair, that they each were of the Chartreux breed.

"Is that... is that *three* of her?" Madeleine exclaimed, her voice was awe made audible. The three identical gray cats cried, mewling as they crept toward their surrogate mother's teats. With her labor complete, the tawny cat turned her attention to eating the afterbirth and chewing apart the remaining umbilical cord. Then she rested as the kittens she had birthed nursed.

"Is it? Is it really three of her?" Madeleine queried again, not able to take her eyes away from the kittens. The biotechnologist wasn't answering. He was observing the newborns. He picked them up, one by one, examining them.

"Well? There was only supposed to be one. Isn't that right?" Madeleine insisted, growing impatient.

"Let the man do his job, Mads," Douglas chimed in. He might have added more but Madeleine made a gag of her glare as she stared her husband into silence.

"Well?" she chided, turning her cold, condemning eyes from her husband to the scientist. She hadn't trusted the man from the start. Hadn't trusted his website, his face, this facility. She hadn't even trusted that the man's name was truly what he purported it to be. But she had been desperate, and he had been willing to give her back her cat when no one else would.

Both a biotechnologist and a veterinary doctor, Dr. Gabriel Gene of Gene Genie Genetics was large bodied, clean shaven, with a shock of slightly salted brown hair. He wore a white coat, a burgundy bowtie, and an expression on his face that led Madeleine to believe he might not know exactly what he was doing. It was the same constantly quizzical expression that had caused her to not trust his face in the first place. The man was altogether quackish.

"It seems... it seems as though the embryo triplicated. That happens from time to time," he said, apparently unconcerned. His hint of a French accent made him sound flippant.

"That *happens* from *time* to *time*?" Madeleine began, indignant, her voice raising a decibel with each syllable she spoke. She paused to inhale. Douglas flinched, took a step back. Dr. Gene's expression went from quizzical to concerned. He raised his hands as though fending off an attack, and from between them he said,

"It happened with Barbra Streisand!"

The mention of the songstress caused Madeleine to calm. In Barbra there would be guidance. In Barbra she trusted. But she was hesitant to trust this man. He hadn't been involved in the cloning of Barbra's dog whatsoever; the company that had done so, as well as every other cloning company Madeleine had reached out to, had declined her request to bring Padmé back. Every one of them had said it couldn't be done. All except for Gene

4

Genie and its proprietor and head biotechnologist, Dr. Gene.

"I mean, it's safe to *assume* that is what happened with Mrs. Streisand," the doctor continued, apparently sensing Madeleine's skepticism. "One way or another, she currently has the care of two full-grown happy and healthy cloned dogs. You can keep all three kittens, but you are under no obligation to. If you choose to leave any of them behind, I promise that they will be taken care of, rest assured."

"Now we have to figure out which *one* to take," Douglas said, speaking in the hesitant way he sometimes spoke when he wasn't sure he should be speaking.

It was a decision Madeleine dreaded. She considered taking all three, but knew, based on his statement, that Douglas only wanted one cat. And even that may have been one too many for his liking. He and Padmé had never exactly gotten along. The cat had belonged to them both but had really been Madeleine's. And Madeleine had been hers. The two had bonded in a nearly symbiotic way. That was what she wanted back, that feeling of her and her best friend. She didn't want a troupe of cats; she only wanted her special little sweetheart.

How to decide? How to decide?

"You don't have to decide this minute," Dr. Gene said, not having to read her thoughts when her indecision was plain to see. "They still need several weeks before they can leave their surrogate. You can check in between now and then and dec–"

A yowl, a hiss; these noises interrupted his statement. The surrogate reared up, hissed again at the kittens she had delivered, and readjusted herself on the birthing bed, walking a few unsteady paces before plopping herself down two feet from where she had previously been, an area which was stained with evidence of her labor – maroon splotches, pieces of umbilical cord, half consumed placenta and fetal membranes. Along with these was a small puddle of fresh blood, bright red upon the white cloth of the bed.

"Did one of them *bite* her?" Douglas asked, alarmed. "Can a kitten even bite?"

"No, it would be highly unlikely. It's more likely that her reaction was the result of discomfort from the birthing process," the doctor said. But he didn't sound certain. Madeleine wasn't certain either as she observed two of the kittens trundle over to the spot of blood and begin to lap it up. The third cat, eyes closed as all kittens' eyes are for days after they are born, seemed to have lost her way and was inching toward the group that had witnessed her entrance to the world, only stopping when she reached the boundary of the birthing bed.

"Maybe we don't have to pick one. It looks like this little lady picked us!" Madeleine declared, delighted, taking a nitrile-gloved index finger and gently stroking the newborn's head. As if wanting to confirm what Madeleine had said, the little kitten did something that startled them all.

She opened her eyes.

Those distinct highlighter yellow eyes Madeleine had loved so much were just as she remembered, only smaller, younger. She burst into tears of joy.

"Welcome back, Padmé!"

"Is everything okay with Padmé?" Madeleine said by way of greeting upon answering the incoming phone call. She had been equal parts anxious and excited to see the name of the person who was calling.

It was two weeks after leaving the facility where the new versions of Padmé had been born. The couple were driving to the country club to take advantage of a perfect afternoon. A day made for golfing or lounging by the pool – blue sky, few clouds, warm with a welcome wind.

Douglas was behind the wheel on one of his many afternoons off from the office – *his* office – where he owned and (occasionally) operated an occupational therapy practice. At this point, over two decades into proprietorship, the place practically ran itself. And did so profitably. Madeleine hadn't worked since before the birth of their eighteen-year-old son, Jaimie.

With her phone linked to the stereo system, the voice on the other end of the line came through the speakers of the *BMW 5 Series*.

"Good afternoon, Mrs. Miller. Yes, everything is okay. Better than okay, depending on how you see things," said Dr. Gene of Gene Genie Genetics.

Madeleine looked over at Douglas. On her husband's face was an expression that mirrored her thoughts: *What does that mean?*

Madeleine had been worried about potential bad news since leaving the Gene Genie facility. The three Padmé clones had been atypical of newborn kittens right from their birth. It turned out that one of the kittens *had* bitten her surrogate mother; bit the nipple of the cat until it had bled. And the Padmé they had chosen, the one who had opened her eyes, she should not have been able to do so. Not so soon after birth.

"What is the issue, doctor?" Madeleine demanded, her heart pounding. Her mind, as it often did when she hadn't yet tamped it down with drink or drug, was involuntarily flashing back to the day she had lost Padmé the first time. The idea of losing her once more after being without her for so long was something Madeleine wouldn't be able to take. She would sue this doctor and his damned facility into inexistence for putting her through such grief.

"No issue. Padmé is ready to go home with you."

"*What!*" Madeleine cried. The sound was birdlike, something between a screech and a squawk. Douglas looked over, briefly taking his eyes from the road to witness Madeleine's beaming smile, a rarity since the day her cat had perished. "We were expecting not to have her for another six weeks!"

Madeleine was laughing, her hands clasped at her modest bosom, her face all eyes as she leaned toward the car's dash. She was a child at a magic show, youth wowed to wonderment. This was the moment she had been waiting for since seeing the interview with Barbra Streisand and her dogs on *Entertainment Tonight*. Since she had found out it was possible to get her beloved cat back. Now, even after the birth, the hefty payments, the paperwork, it finally felt real. Padmé was coming back home.

"Yes..." the doctor said. The hesitation in his voice tempered Madeleine. She sat back in her seat, wow and wonderment withered. "We are a bit ahead of schedule with their growth. I don't want you to be alarmed when you see them..."

But the mention of potential alarm set alarm bells ringing for Madeleine, her mind now pandemonium.

"What do you mean?"

"Uhh," said the doctor. "Perhaps it's best you see for yourself when you get here."

"Accelerated growth program?" Douglas asked, perplexed. Madeleine said nothing. She only scowled at the scientist in front of them as he attempted to explain away the mistake he had made. An explanation she was, so far, finding unacceptable.

They were within the facility. Inside the manmade mar in an otherwise beautiful natural surrounding. A building two tones of gray in the midst of lush leaves, brown branches, green grasses, and brightly colored bloom. They had cut across cities, raced by the countryside, driven to this wooded seclusion, in order to get their cat. To see what might be wrong with her.

Upon arrival, nearly two hours after receiving Dr. Gene's call, they had rushed past the receptionist, who hissed for them to come back, to declare their business, to state their reason for being there. Ignoring the receptionist, they had burst into the doctor's office, interrupting his midday meal – some sort of sandwich, the contents of which seemed to be as much spilled on his desk as stuffed into his gullet. Cleaning his chin with a napkin before using that napkin to cover the mess on his desk, he had called for calm. When some measure of it was found, he had asked for them to follow him.

Dr. Gene had led the distressed couple down the corridor to one of the many rooms filled with caged cats and dogs, gerbils and ferrets, pets of all nature. Most of them, Madeleine assumed, had to be clones.

They were taken to one of the glass cells recessed within the wall, not unlike those of a pet store. There, in the enclosure, were the three Chartreux kittens. One of those gray, yellow-eyed cats had a pink collar around her neck. That collared kitten was their Padmé.

There was, thankfully, nothing wrong with the kittens physically. The triplicates were healthy, hale, and seemingly happy as they pawed at and played with one another. They were all in good form.

The issue, the reason the doctor had brought them there, warned them, the reason that had made Madeleine mad, was that the three Chartreux kittens were each twice the size they ought to have been. If Madeleine hadn't witnessed them being born only two weeks prior, she would have sworn they were approaching two months old.

"Yes," Dr. Gene replied slowly, hesitantly, regarding Madeleine and her madwoman's glare even though the question had been asked by Douglas. "The accelerated growth program is not yet available to the public. You know, government regulations and conditions, FDA assessments, red tape, red tape, red tape. But the gist of it is: we have found a way to reunite pet owners with the pets they remember even faster than before. Everyone wants a clone, yes?" He looked for them to agree, but both only stared at the man, Douglas confused, Madeleine concerned.

"Yes," the doctor said, answering himself. "And though many owners appreciate the time spent with their kittens and puppies and what-have-you – raising the babies all over again – most owners are eager to be with their pets as they remember them when they died... Or shortly prior, depending on the condition of the pet at death, of course." He looked apologetically at Madeleine as he said this. "These people come here hoping for the sort of cloning one has seen in the movies – an animal or person steps into one machine, and out of another machine, like a xeroxed sheet of paper, comes an identical copy, exactly as is. While we are not quite yet able to do such a thing at this point, we here at Gene Genie Genetics have gotten one step closer. And, thus, one step ahead of our competitors in the industry. Which means you, Mrs. and Mr.

Miller, are one step closer to being with the version of Padmé you knew and loved for so many years."

He was selling as he was speaking, a businessman and a biotechnologist, a marketer and man of science. And Madeleine found, to her surprise, that she was accepting the explanation offered, she was buying what he sold.

"In order to accommodate this want of the customer, we are able to accelerate the growth process. From infancy to adulthood in a matter of months. A much more expedited reuniting of pet and owner. We expect, once our process is officially approved in the not-too-distant future and we are allowed to offer it to patrons, that this particular innovation will be the most popular option in cloning technology anywhere around the globe. This is a revolution, Mrs. Miller! And you, through our error, for which I do profusely apologize, are first in line to experience the dawn of the future, the rise of a whole new path of pet ownership! A revolution!"

"Yes, yes, a revolution. You've said that once already," Madeleine replied, her hard expression slightly softer, though still stony, as she regarded the scientist. She looked from him to a python in an enclosure across the room, then to a quartet of identical black bunnies in another, a bunch of baby basset hounds in a third.

"Will they die faster?" Madeleine asked, when her eyes returned to the cluster of kittens in question. "Will the accelerated clones die before the other clones or regular kittens? You know, grow faster, die faster. That's what I'm asking."

"That, Mrs. Miller, is the beauty of our process. Padmé will have her full life expectancy. Our trials have seen tremendous successes thus far. Incredible results! So, while this error of ours – running Padmé's DNA through our trial process instead of our standard cloning process – was a mistake, it may also be a small miracle. You'll have your Padmé back quick as a whip. And, of course, at no extra charge to you."

Madeleine raised an eyebrow, pursed her lips, made an expression that let Dr. Gene know that *he* was lucky *they* wouldn't be charging *him* for his mistake. Charging him by way of a lawsuit. But he only smiled back in return, part of his lunch – a bit of greenery – still stuck between his teeth. He was a salesman aware that the deal was done. There was nothing she wanted more than to be back with her Padmé. She would never explicitly state it, but she was glad for the mistake.

"What's next?" she asked.

"You're okay with this?" Douglas inquired of her. Being an unwitting part of an unapproved experiment likely wasn't increasing his optimism about a process he had already been hesitant to partake in.

"I am," Madeleine said, never taking her eyes away from the smiling scientist. "So long as the gene genie here gives us his assurances that Padmé will be healthy and normal."

"I assure you," replied the doctor without pause, his smile fading, his face all solemnity. "The government approval is just a formality at this point. Our trials have been remarkable. Padmé is as healthy as any cat can be. And she will remain so. I promise you, Mrs. and Mr. Miller, nothing will go wrong."

"We're home!" Madeleine sang into the house. Her arms were full of her long-lost cat as she walked through the front door, which was being held open by her husband. She was cradling the swaddled Chartreux kitten as she would a new-born baby. Though the word "kitten" might not apply to Padmé for much longer if her accelerated growth went as the doctor had projected.

"Jaimie! Come re-meet your little sister!" Madeleine called cheerily from the foyer, raising her face and her voice toward the upper level of the house. Her son and only child (other than Padmé, of course) was likely in his bedroom playing those internet games or watching that internet pornography. The internet, she lamented, had ruined the child. Madeleine was hoping Padmé would bring her nearly adult son out of his yearslong lull.

Twelve years ago, when she had originally invited him to meet his little sister, her then six-year-old boy had run from his nanny and had practically stormed his mother and the kitten she had arrived home with, grinning and giggling all the while. The excitement he had displayed that special day had rarely been rivalled throughout his years since. Where had her happy child gone? she wondered, as she heard his bedroom door open, his heavy steps approach. Watched him appear at the railing of the second floor. He did not storm her. There was no joyous grin nor gleeful giggle. He only glared. In his black clothes, through his black expression, he said,

"Keep that fucking thing away from me."

"Jaimie!" Douglas roared at their son. "Don't you talk to your mother that way! You come down here and see Paddy. Your mom has been excited about this for a long time, and you're ruining it!"

"Paddy is dead, dad! And whatever the fuck that creature is, it isn't her! And it won't change what mom did to her!" That stated, Jaimie retreated into his dank, smelly lair of a bedroom.

The Madeleine of two months ago would have been damaged by the interaction. But that iteration of Madeleine had been without sweet baby Padmé. Now, with her kitten in her arms, Jaimie's latest outburst was only a papercut rather than the stab wound she was accustomed to them being.

"Jaimie! You come back here and apologize to your mother this instant!"

"No, no, it's okay," Madeleine said, whispered the words. But she wasn't speaking to her husband, not directly. She was speaking to the little bundle of joy in her arms. "It's okay. Everything is okay now that we have Padmé back. Everything is just absolutely perfect."

"God! When is she going to learn? You can't trust those damn DiMeras," an exasperated Madeleine said to Padmé as the two sat on the couch watching an episode of *Days of Our Lives*. Padmé was indifferent to the events on the television screen. The cat was curled up, a small gray ball pressed against her owner's thigh. It was almost exactly as it had been.

Three months after the birth of the cloned cat, Madeleine and Padmé had settled into their old routine, spending their days together on the living room couch watching soap operas, or chatting in one of the neighborhood's many Facebook groups. She had done these things without Padmé, but they had felt empty, hollow, as had she. And that was the reason her drinking had gotten worse.

She had, prior to the tragedy of Padmé's end, enjoyed a glass or two of red wine with her lunch, another couple before her husband got home from work or running errands. But after Padmé's death, that one or two glasses by lunchtime had turned into one or two bottles.

Then there were the pills. Those grief-relieving little bits of magic in the form of a tablet or a capsule. A neighbor had recommended and supplied Madeleine with valium and pain killers to help dull the sharp edge that was her endless mourning shortly after Padmé's passing. She had been taking them every few hours ever since. And though, right now, she was drunk on wine, and though, right now, she was high on pills, she thought that, with Padmé by her side, she could cut back. In a while. If she wanted to.

Madeleine heard the front door open. She looked at the clock on the wall above the ninety-inch flat screen television. Four o'clock. Douglas was right on time as always.

"You awake, hon?" he called into the house. Madeleine had taken to taking long afternoon naps. She often woke in the evening with her husband home, her dinner made, and a full glass of wine waiting for her at the table.

"Yes, darling. Padmé and I are just watching TV." She paused the episode. On the screen, an elderly John Black and Marlena Evans were reuniting for what had to be the thousandth time. Madeleine smiled at the couple. She would never get tired of those two.

"In the mood for steak?" Douglas said sunnily, poking his smiling head into the living room. He was holding up a brown paper bag from the butcher a few blocks away. Before waiting for her to respond, he upped the ante. Stepping full into the doorway, he showed her what was in his other hand. "How about a bottle of Château Margaux to go with it!" he declared, feigning a French accent. It was the same voice he put on when imitating Dr. Gene.

"Ohh!" She straightened in her seat, squealed, and clapped, startling Padmé and sending the cat clambering off the couch and out of the room.

"There goes Paddy!" Douglas said. They both laughed. Things felt right again. Just as they once had. Until Douglas said something that reminded Madeleine that things weren't quite the same. That Padmé wasn't quite the same.

"Has she gotten even bigger since this morning?"

"Ugh. I hope not. She's getting so big so quickly. I thought I would like the whole accelerated growth thing, but I forgot how much I loved her as a kitten." She stuck out her bottom lip, pouting in exaggerated fashion. "How did you get the Margaux? Frederick said they wouldn't have another shipment in for months!"

"I know a guy," Douglas responded with a wink. "One of my longtime clients took a vacation to France. I greased his palms a bit and told him to bring me back a bottle. Just for you." He had walked into the living room while speaking, made his way toward his wife, and punctuated his sentence with a kiss on her lips.

"What's the occasion?" she asked, after they parted. He placed the bottle of Pavillon Rouge du Château Margaux on the black marble coffee table. "Or are you just trying to get laid again?" She gave him a wink and a slight slap on the bottom. Again, they both laughed.

Their sex life was much improved in the months since her cat had been resurrected (for that was how Madeleine thought of it). After Padmé's death, she hadn't cared much for her husband's touch. Hadn't had the energy or patience to make the best of his mediocre lovemaking. She couldn't will herself, as she previously had, to cheer him on with practiced moans or groans or well timed whimpers as he pumped and pawed for the few minutes he would last. More and more, it had been him stealing time with his hand; and she with her toys and plugs and vibrating things on the rare occasion the mood struck her.

But with the resurrection of Padmé had come the reignition of a love life that had been smothered, nearly outed entirely by grief. Now, grief gone, loins and libidos relit, they burned for each other as they had in their college days. And every once in a while, when he was motivated and she was the right balance of drunk and high, the sex was as good as it had been back then.

"No occasion. Except it's good to have you back again. And that's all thanks to Padm—Hey!"

The cat he had been about to commend had crept back into the room while the couple was kissing and carrying on. Padmé had taken an interest in the brown bag full of meat, pouncing on it as Douglas was speaking. Nearly wrenching it from his grip.

"Stop it, Paddy!" Douglas said, holding tight to the twisted twine handles, trying his best to rip the steaks free from Padmé's pursuing paws. The cat's nails were stabbing into the paper bag, she was biting down on it as well. Madeleine observed in hushed horror as her husband and her cat engaged in a tug of war over the slabs of beef.

The bag tore. Douglas fell backward. He would have crashed onto the floor if the loveseat hadn't caught him. The bag split, and from it spilled three uncooked steaks wrapped in butcher paper.

"Damnit!" Douglas yelled. Madeleine said nothing, only watched as her cat pounced on the steak which had fallen nearest her. Tearing through the butcher paper, she was a child on Christmas morning. And it was apparent to Madeleine, given the ferocity with which the cat had begun to feed on the well marbled ribeye, that no one was going to take this gift away from her. Yet Douglas tried.

Now back on his feet, having practically leapt from the loveseat to the spot where Padmé fed, Douglas reached down, went to grab the steak Padmé was occupied with. And that was when the cat reacted.

Madeleine barely saw it; Padmé's paw became a gray streak, a near-black blur. Douglas cried out, stood erect, stepped back, stumbled, nearly fell again but managed to maintain his feet while he clutched his hand to his chest. He looked at Madeleine with the expression one might find on the face of a child who has discovered, for the first time, the feeling of a hot stove. It was an expression of betrayal, of misunderstanding. And then of disgust as Douglas looked down and saw that the back of his right hand was bleeding heavily.

"That fucking thing *gouged* me!"

"Hey! Don't you talk about Padmé like that! She didn't mean to!" Madeleine exclaimed, now rising from the couch to physically step between her husband and her cat.

"That's *not* Pad..." Douglas began. But he froze when he saw the way his wife's face contorted as he had started to respond; an arching of a brow, a clenching of her jaw, a twisting of her lips.

"Don't. Don't you say that."

"But Madeleine! We have to be realistic! This isn't the first time she's done something like this!" It was true. Loathe to admit it as Madeleine was, this version of Padmé (and she hated to think of her as just a *version* of Padmé, and not the same creature reincarnated) was more aggressive than the original Padmé had been. This change in temperament usually came about when someone attempted to touch her or tamper with the object of her focus when Padmé was eating or otherwise occupied. Both Douglas and Madeleine had been bitten and scratched previously, but the damage done then was nothing to his latest lacerations.

He had untucked his shirt and was pressing the material against his hand to stop the bleeding. To no avail. Madeleine could see the blood dyeing the pale blue shirt red, staining it. As the stain spread and grew, so too did the couple's rift.

"The doctor said it would take time for her to adjust. The doctor said that we couldn't expect her to be the exact same because she wouldn't have the exact same experiences. The doctor sai–"

"Did the doctor say she was going to turn into a dangerous little asshole?" Douglas whined.

"*Douglas!*"

"It's true, Mads! This cat just isn't th–"

26

"Douglas. *Stop!*"

"We have to be honest with ours–"

"Not another word!"

"That is n–"

"*I said not another word!*" Madeleine shrieked. Her hands made fists, those fists rose to her ears and covered them as she screamed at her husband. He heeded her, didn't say another word. In the space where words weren't spoken, a sound other than those made by the quarrelling couple finally registered to Madeleine. It was the sound of Padmé feasting, and it was a disconcerting noise.

She didn't immediately turn around to look upon her cat. She only stared at her husband's dismayed face, seeing there all she needed to know. He didn't say another word, not with his mouth. But with the rest of his face, his eyes, with the language of his body, she could hear him clearly. *If that's your cat then explain what she is doing*, was what she read from her husband. *If that's the same Padmé then why won't you turn around and face her?*

Madeleine did turn, slowly, ever so slowly, to face the source of the sounds of ripping, rending. By the time she had completed the 180-degree spin, the sounds of her cat's feast were done. Because Padmé was done with the steak that had fallen in front of her.

In the span of Mr. and Mrs. Miller's brief row, the entire slab of meat had been consumed. The only evidence of it remaining was shredded butcher paper, a small clean cylindrical bone, and several stains on the cream-colored carpet; leftover blood that Padmé was quietly licking up.

"A protein deficiency?" Douglas asked.

"A *severe* protein deficiency," Madeleine reiterated happily, not long after ending the phone call she had been on with Dr. Gene. She was relieved to have an answer regarding Padmé's appetite and agitation when it came to the steak she had stolen from Douglas. A rational, scientific explanation, rather than her son's assertion that the scientist and his facility had created a cat-sized Monster of Frankenstein.

The Millers (minus Jaimie, who only ate in his room) were at their dining table, eating the Chinese food they had ordered in. Neither of them was in the mood for the remaining steak or anything remotely close to it after what had happened earlier that day.

"I don't know, Mads," Douglas said with a sigh, a fork full of chow mein suspended in stasis between his plate and his mouth. "It seems like that doctor has a clever explanation for everything."

"Well, I would think that just about every explanation for something as complex as cloning would have to be clever, wouldn't you?" Madeleine responded with an edge to her voice, a change in her tone that let Douglas know she wouldn't accept his naysaying. "But it *does* make sense. The accelerated clones grow faster than normal cats, so they need more protein than normal cats. And cats are carnivores, remember? Poor Padmé was probably just starved for it, and that's why she went after the steaks."

"But..." Douglas began. Madeleine glared him into acceptance. It was the way most of their arguments went.

"She'll be fine. We just have to get used to a few differences and account for some adjustments." Those were Dr. Gene's words, and Madeleine was making of them a mantra, needing to do so to quell her own concerns. She looked around for Padmé, as if seeing the cat would calm her, would remind her that things were fine. Just fine. But Padmé wasn't in the kitchen. She hoped the cat hadn't been scared too badly after having to fight Douglas for the protein she sorely needed. Madeleine did her best to put her concerns out of her mind, reminding herself again of the biotechnologist's words.

"So…" she said, changing the subject after swallowing a bite of a spring roll she thought to be utterly tasteless. "How was your d–"

A shriek from upstairs disrupted her question.

"Jaimie!" the couple said simultaneously as they stood, as if synchronized, from their seats.

Another scream from their son.

Again, in unison, they abandoned their meals and ran toward the cries of their child.

🐈 🐈 🐈 🐈 🐈 🐈 🐈

"I told you to keep that fucking thing away from me!" Jaimie said to his parents after they had made their way up the stairs and found him standing in the doorway of his bathroom. He was naked aside from the towel wrapped around his waist.

Madeleine followed his accusatory stare to the end of the hall where Padmé sat, staring back, clearly shaken.

"Look!" Jaimie yelled, before Madeleine could ask what the matter was. She turned to him, to his face, then to his finger pointing down at his foot; at what he wanted her and Douglas to see.

"I can relate," Douglas commiserated, gesturing with his head to his bandaged hand. On Jaimie's foot were three gouges, blood running from them each and mixing with the water that was beaded on his body.

"What happened?" Madeleine asked her son as steam from the bathroom seeped out of the doorway around him, mixing with the steam rising from him, from his rage.

"I was in the shower, and I heard someone at the door. I thought it was one of you with how loud it was. I thought something was wrong! When I opened the door, that little fucking Frankenstein scratched me!"

"Jaimie!" Madeleine cried. "That is *Padmé*. Your little sister! She was only trying to play with you! Just like old times."

Jaimie, his entire face furled, drew in a sharp breath, making a sound akin to a hiss. And like the animal most associated with that sound, he looked ready to unleash venom. He opened his mouth but stopped before he spoke. Something in his eyes softened as he looked at his mother. It was as though he only truly saw her for the first time. As though he hadn't recognized her until just now.

"Mom... I understand you can't forgive yourself for what happened to Paddy... I know I haven't given you the easiest time about it. But this is *too* far. Don't you *see* that? You can't bring her back." He looked down the hall, to Padmé, who sat there watching them, bright eyes unblinking. "Even bringing her back can't bring her back."

"But she *is* back. Can't *you* see that? She's right there. She's still her," Madeleine insisted while waving warmly at the cat. "Right, Padmé? You're still my sweet little lady, aren't you?"

She spoke to her feline friend in the slow, high-pitched tone that can only be produced when induced by small children or cute animals. Padmé meowed the way she always had when addressed by her name. And that was proof enough for Madeleine.

"See?" she insisted to her son.

Jaimie rolled his eyes until they turned from his mother to his father.

"Are you really going to keep letting her delude herself?"

Douglas looked at the floor, at every inch of it, it seemed, before he responded.

"Your mom is happy now. That's all that matters, son."

Jaimie, his face furrowed even further, scoffed at his father's words, released another hiss. And here it came, the venom:

"*Son?*" Jaimie said to his father, mocking Douglas' voice. "Are you sure about that? I thought you had to have a pair of balls to be able to reproduce."

"*Jaimie!*"

"Save it, mom! I don't want to hear it! There's something seriously wrong with that thing. Whatever it is, it's not Paddy. And it wasn't trying to play with me 'just like old times.'" He mimicked his mother with the finishing of that sentence. Made her sound petulant, pathetic, pitiful. "And if you don't believe that, just look at what it did." He waved his hand downward, once more guiding their eyes to follow its movement. When they looked down, he stepped back into the bathroom, closed the door between them.

Initially, Madeleine believed her son had gestured to the blood on the floor. It had flowed from his lacerations and mixed with the water that had dripped from him. The resulting puddles were light red, nearly pink.

"Oh God," Douglas whispered. He saw it first. It wasn't the blood Jaimie had gestured to. It was the door he had closed. The base of it. Madeleine had no words upon sight of the revelation. She held a hand to her mouth while turning from the door to the cat. Padmé, no longer watching Madeleine and Douglas, was grooming herself.

Had Madeleine's sweet little angel really done such damage?

At the base of the door were scratches, claw marks, grooves. They didn't look like the markings of a playful companion but the work of a feral beast. An animal intent on entry. One that – based on the depth and number of claw marks – might have eventually been able to tunnel through the door had it not been opened by Jaimie.

Madeleine looked to Douglas, met his eyes, saw the horror in them. She turned back to Padmé, who only continued to clean herself, mindless of all around her.

The cat was paying special attention to her paws and claws, from which she was licking the paint, the wood shavings, she had scraped from the bathroom door. And the blood, which she had extracted from their son.

"I think something *is* wrong with Padmé," Madeleine begrudgingly admitted to Douglas as the two prepared for bed.

It was hours after the confrontation with Jaimie and the discovery of the damage to the door. She was no less shaken by what had occurred, unable to think of anything else all night. It pained her to believe that her son might be correct. That the decision to bring Padmé back could have been a mistake.

Douglas emerged from the bathroom adjoining their bedroom, teeth freshly brushed, while Madeleine was crouched in the corner by the closet where Padmé rested – just as she always had – on the towel that Madeleine had placed on that same spot over a decade ago. Save for washing it on occasion, that plush pink towel had remained there. After Padmé had passed on, Madeleine had not allowed it to be moved. And now here was Padmé, on top of it, back where she belonged. But something was not right.

"What's wrong? What's the matter?" Douglas asked from across the room.

"It's her stomach," Madeleine said, standing up after petting the cat a final time. Padmé grumbled, shifted with discomfort. She was on her side, showing her belly, which had become distended at some point during the evening. Something in that swollen stomach seemed to shift. "I think..." Madeleine didn't want to say it, could barely force herself to. "I think it's cancer."

"*What?*" Douglas said, alarmed, and alarming her because he spoke from right beside her when she had expected him to still be by the bathroom door. Slightly shaken, she turned to her husband who was looking at Padmé's stomach. "What makes you think she has cancer?" he asked.

Madeleine was no scientist, but she knew enough about cell growth to put together a hypothesis based on the swollen stomach of her cat.

"The doctor said that the new program of theirs makes pets age faster due to accelerated cell growth, right? Well, cancer is a cell. What if one of her cells became cancerous and now it's growing just as quickly as everything else?" She looked at Padmé's bloated belly. "Or maybe even quicker than everything else."

Her imagination took her to darknesses she would rather not attend. She envisioned waking up in the morning to open tumors all over her cat's body, an exploded stomach. She pictured Padmé dead again, though in a much different fashion than the first time. It was an idea she couldn't bear.

"You sure it's not just gas from all the steak she ate earlier? Not to mention the chunks she took out of me and Jaimie." He gave her a bashful look that indicated he was half joking. Madeleine was maudlin while modelling a maddened expression on her face that said she was entirely serious. She had no room for humor. Not when Padmé was in pain. Douglas sighed, tentatively touched his wife on the shoulder. When he found that his head was still attached to his body, he put his arm around her. He kissed her on the cheek.

"Tomorrow, honey, I'll take the afternoon off, and we'll take her back to Dr. Gene. We'll get some straight answers out of that quack."

"Tomorrow," Madeleine repeated, walking slowly to the bed. Lying in it, closing her eyes. "Tomorrow. Okay," she whispered, before the sedative that was wine and valium began to put her under.

"Tomorrow, yes. Padmé will be better in the morning," Douglas reassured. That was the last thing she heard from her husband. She fell asleep wanting to believe him.

But when morning came, when it was tomorrow, Padmé was nowhere to be found.

🐈 🐈 🐈 🐈 🐈 🐈 🐈 🐈 🐈

"Padmé! Padmé! Where are you?" Madeleine cried out into her empty house, desperately, despondently.

It was happening again. Madeleine's worst nightmare. Padmé missing. Padmé gone.

Douglas wasn't there either. He had an important meeting that morning and wouldn't be returning until past noon.

"I'm sure she's just hiding. I'll be back in a jiff," he had said, before rushing out the door. A part of her wondered if he hadn't been glad to have that meeting. She was sure he was happy to avoid everything going on. Meanwhile, Jaimie was at school; not a goodbye, not a word, before he had left.

She was alone now. As she had been alone on the day of Padmé's death.

Both days were meshing, this and that grim afternoon. She was in a daze of déjà vu. Two timelines that should not have intertwined were now twisting, becoming braided. That bad day bursting into this one. The memory she had been able to dampen with her drinking and her drugs was roaring back full force.

She remembered, just over two years ago, going out to the back yard to have a smoke and a chat on the phone. It was a scandal. The affair between her neighbors, Jeanie Caruso and Kendal Kelsey had been exposed. It was an entanglement everyone except for Kendal's husband had already suspected or known. Madeleine had walked onto the back deck, a glass of red liquid, full to the brim, in her left hand, a cigarette burning in her mouth, licentious rumors smoldering in her ear as she lay on her deck chair.

She hadn't realized she had left the back door open. Hadn't seen Padmé, a lifelong indoor cat, run out of the house, around the side of it.

An hour passed before, sun-kissed and tipsy, Madeleine stumbled into the house and called happily for her cat. Padmé never answered. Never would.

Another hour passed as she searched her home before remembering the unclosed door, the chance that Padmé, who had never so much as stepped on a blade of grass, was now outside, a house cat in a wild world.

Madeleine had run into the back yard. Calling. Calling. Crying. She had run around the side of the house, her head twisting in all directions, the world a cat-less blur. Then, when Madeleine had focused on the road in front of her house, she had seen her.

Padmé.

In the street.

Padmé.

Nearly bifurcated.

"Padmé!"

A car had run her best friend down. Over. And had kept on rolling.

Madeleine had sprinted into the street on that sunny afternoon, had run to the corpse of her fur baby. And had scooped Padmé up, struggling to keep her cat's remains intact as she did so.

The neighbors had found her there, on her knees, howling at the sky, clutching something barely recognizable as her longtime household pet.

It had been misery after that. Until Madeleine had watched that very special episode of *Entertainment Tonight* featuring Barbra Streisand and her dogs. By then, Padmé had been gone for a year and a half. And that, the duration since her death, had been the greatest obstacle when it came to bringing her back to life.

After watching Barbra's interview about her dogs, Madeleine had contacted cloning companies all over the country, and several overseas in Europe and Asia. Every place she had researched and emailed and called had told her the same thing: they couldn't clone a cat that had been dead for almost two years; the requisite genetic material had to be gathered within five days of the animal's expiration. Madeleine had refused to give up. It wasn't until she was at her most desperate, in a state of renewed mourning, that she had reached out to a facility she had originally overlooked. Gene Genie Genetics, the company was called.

She hadn't liked the name of it, nor the unprofessional look of their website, nor the unprofessional look of the man pictured on said site. Dr. Gabriel Gene, who was listed as proprietor, veterinary doctor, and principal biotechnologist, had been photoshopped on the website's homepage into a blue genie emerging from a beaker instead of a magic lamp. The mist that made up the portion of the genie wafting out of the beaker formed a double helix. She had considered the place to be a nonstarter until all her options had stopped. Madeleine had been in despair, and Gene Genie had been close, and so she had called.

"Not with the hair," the doctor had said, in a hushed tone after he had initially declined her request. She had implored him to reconsider, to consider it at all, insisting she had plenty of the cat's hair that could be used to extract Padmé's DNA. "Not with *only* the hair, though it might help. We are working on a few innovative cloning techniques here. It will cost you a little extra above our more typical procedure, but if you could, perhaps, and pardon me for the grim nature of my request... but if you could bring in your little cat's bones, maybe something can be done..."

She had more than pardoned him for his request, she had thanked him, ecstatic, counting her blessings that she had declined her veterinarian's offer of cremation after Padmé's death.

She had told Douglas her plan that same afternoon. Mr. Miller had hummed and hawed, had huffed his hesitancy. But, as he almost always did, Douglas had acquiesced. The following morning, he paid their gardener a hefty bonus to exhume Padmé's corpse from its grave in the corner of their backyard, beneath the apple tree.

With the tiny coffin, with every hair she could pluck from the cat's old towel and toys, with every portion of Padmé that could possibly be procured, Madeleine and Douglas had gone to the Gene Genie facility. Several months later, Padmé had been reborn. And reborn and reborn.

Madeleine did her best to shake the memory of what had started this entire ordeal from her mind now as she continued the search for her cat. It was the third time she had checked her home, everywhere from the wine cellar to the attic. The last spot she surveyed, on this most recent turn, was the back of the fridge. Again, Padmé wasn't there. Again, Padmé was nowhere.

Exasperated, exhausted, Madeleine knew what she had to do. She had to leave the house and check the street. See if Padmé had wandered outside again somehow.

She walked to the front door, stood there, hesitant to open it. If she looked out at the street and saw what she had seen the last time, her mind might never recover. But she had to check, had to know.

"Padmé!" she wailed mournfully, as she grabbed the knob, prepared to twist, braced herself for what she might see once the door was open.

But Padmé stopped her.

From somewhere in the house, the cat meowed.

"Padmé?" Madeleine cried out, not quite believing her ears. Another responsive meow came from upstairs.

Madeleine hadn't run so quickly since her high school days. She took the stairs two at a time, nearly leaping up to the second floor landing, calling out to Padmé and following the cat's replies. The meowing led Madeleine into her bedroom, to her closet. The door was ajar. She opened it fully. Entered.

And saw nothing but their clothes, her shoes. No cat.

"Padmé?"

The meow again, from behind one of the shoe racks.

"Oh Padmé! Why were you hiding from me?"

Madeleine walked further into the closet, toward one of the three racks of shoes running along each wall. In the corner, between two of those cubby style racks, hidden out of sight by their protrusion, was Padmé. And Madeleine immediately saw why the cat had been hiding.

"Oh..." she uttered unbelievingly. "How?"

For a time, she only stood there, frozen in astonishment at the sight before her. Eventually, after thawing from her surprise, she reached into her pocket for her phone. Called her husband, who answered after barely a ring.

"Douglas... I found her."

"That's amazing, honey! How is she? Where was she?"

"Douglas..." Madeleine wasn't sure how to say it. Because it didn't make sense. "She wasn't alone when I found her."

"What do you mean? Are *you* okay?"

She wasn't okay. She was shaken. Shaking.

"It wasn't a tumor that was the matter with her yesterday. It was... She was pregnant last night, Douglas. That's what was wrong with her stomach."

"*What?* That's crazy. That's not possible!"

Madeleine, on any other day, under any other circumstance, would have agreed. But she was presently perceiving the impossible. In front of her was Padmé. Around Padmé was a litter of kittens. Nine of them. And each of those newborn cats had their eyes open. They were watching Madeleine intently.

"I'm looking at nine kittens, Douglas..."

All of them were charcoal gray.

All of them had the same highlighter yellow eyes.

"And all of them are her."

"Come on, Douglas... Come on, Douglas...
Come on, Douglas..." Madeleine muttered to
herself as she paced the kitchen floor, a glass
of wine in one hand, her phone in the other,
waiting for Douglas' call. She saw through the
kitchen window, with some concern, that the
sun was nearly fully set.

When he had returned home from his
meeting earlier that afternoon, it was decided
that they would call the doctor, demand
answers. They would see what was to be done
about the ten versions of Padmé they were
currently in ownership of.

Douglas and Madeleine had attempted to
contact the scientist for hours. Several times
they tried but hadn't been able to reach Dr.
Gene. When it was clear they would get no
response, Douglas had loaded the kittens into
Padmé's cat carrier and had driven the
newborns to the Gene Genie facility,
determined to get some answers directly,
either from the doctor or any of his staff. He
had wanted to take Padmé, too; to take her

there and leave her there. But Madeleine would not hear of it. Against the advice of her husband, Madeleine had decided to stay and care for Padmé until they got some answers. If they had to give the cat away after those answers were attained, they would deal with that when the time came.

Now, Madeleine, pacing, impatient, still wanting those answers, called the doctor again. Left another angry voicemail.

"You motherfucking fraud! You better not be avoiding us! We'll sue you into the ground for what you've done to Padmé!"

It was the sixteenth such message she had left since discovering Padmé had given birth. Given birth without ever having left the house. Had a litter of kittens without ever having interacted with another cat, other than her littermates and surrogate mother. Had reproduced after she had been spayed. She was the Virgin Mary of felines.

"Are you ready to admit that this was a mistake?" The unexpected voice from behind her caused Madeleine to jolt. Her jolting caused her to spill red wine on her beige blouse.

"Goddammit!" she screamed. She placed the diminished glass of wine on the counter and whirled around to face her son. Jaimie had returned home from whatever it was he did after school not long ago.

"This isn't the time for your shit, Jaimie! You want to say 'I told you so' so badly, then go ahead and say it. I'm not going to argue with you. If your prize is my being unhappy, then here you are, you've won it! *You've won!* Okay? *Okay?*" She broke down then.

It wasn't supposed to be like this, she thought, as she leaned against the kitchen counter and bawled into her hands. It was supposed to be simple, like with Barbra Streisand and her dogs. All Madeleine had wanted was her cat back, and now everything was falling apart!

"Oh!" she cried, when she felt arms wrap around her. She couldn't bring herself to say anything else as her son embraced her for the first time in years. She wept onto his chest, remembering the days when he had been small enough to weep onto hers. How had he gotten so tall so fast? How had she missed so much?

"You need help, mom. This isn't about me winning. This is about you realizing that," Jaimie whispered to her, his lips brushing against the hair above her ear.

And when had he gotten so smart?

She couldn't forge a response, her sobs stealing any chance at speech. Jaimie, content having said his piece, didn't wait for a reply. He gave her a look that showed the concern he felt for her, then left the kitchen, walked down the hall and up the stairs.

Madeleine slid down the cabinet to the floor, still sobbing, though not entirely sure why. She remained there a while, alone, until she received some unexpected company.

A meow made her raise her face from her hands. Padmé was in front of her, looking at her almost quizzically. It was impossible to tell that the cat had given birth only hours earlier. For the first time since bringing Padmé back home, she wasn't sure how to respond to the little creature. A part of Madeleine wanted to scoop the cat into her arms, snuggle up with her as she always would have at any time before this. Another part wanted to shoo her pet away, and that only made her sadder.

"Oh Padmé..." she began. But the ringing of her phone disrupted her sentence and made her decision for her. Padmé ran off, down the hall in the direction Jaimie had gone, when Madeleine flinched at the sound of her phone. Her nerves were on edge. She reminded herself to take another couple of pills when she got up off the floor.

"Douglas!" she answered, relieved to have seen his name on the display. "What did that asshole have to say for himself?"

"Madeleine..." Douglas practically panted into the phone. His voice sounded heavy, burdened by the weight of bad news. "I think Dr. Gene is dead."

"Dead? What? What's going on, Douglas?"

"I think I'm looking at his body right now," he added, sounding shellshocked.

"*You think?* You're not making any sense."

"I'm looking at a dead body, Madeleine. In the facility. But I can't tell a hundred percent if it's the doctor because the face is... the face isn't there anymore. And the body... Christ, Madeleine, I think some of the animals were eating him!" His voice broke. She realized he had been attempting to maintain his composure for her sake. He was panicked. He was terrified. She heard him walking, his footfalls echoing in the building he was in. The further he moved into the facility, the more fearful she felt.

"Get out of there, Douglas! *Right now!* Call the police and get out of there this instant!"

"I don't think anyone else is here. All the enclosures with the pets we saw, they're empty. I think they've all esca– oh God!"

"Douglas!"

"Oh Jesus! No! No! No! Mads! Madeleine! There's so many of them. There's so much blood! Call the police, Mads! And for the love of God, stay away from Pa–"

Screeches. Screams. The dropping of a phone.

Then silence.

"Douglas?"

No response.

"Douglas!"

Dead air.

"DOUG!"

But he was gone. And his screams, Madeleine feared, would be the last thing she would ever hear from her husband.

🐈 🐈 🐈 🐈 🐈 🐈 🐈 🐈 🐈 🐈 🐈

"9-1-1. What's your emergency?"

"My husband! My husband, Douglas. He's in trouble. He's..." She did her best to provide the address of the facility. To let the operator know that something had gone wrong there, that her husband was in danger.

"Okay, ma'am. Try your best to stay calm. Officers will be at the scene in a matter of minutes. In the meanwhile, I would like you to..."

The operator continued to speak, but Madeleine was no longer listening. She thought she heard Jaimie crying out for her, the sound dampened by doors and distance and the wine and pills comingling in her system. She focused, strained to hear him, then she did.

"Mom! Moooom! *Mommy! Help me! Mommy help!*" After that, there was only shrieking.

Forgetting she was on the phone with someone who might have been able to help her son, Madeleine dropped her device. And for the second time in twenty-four hours, she sprinted to the flight of stairs, nearly leaping up them as she followed the sound of Jaimie's panicked voice.

🐈🐈🐈🐈🐈🐈🐈🐈🐈🐈🐈🐈

"Jaimie! Jaimie are you okay?"

There was no response. By the time Madeleine had made it halfway up the stairs, all was quiet. Just like that. Jaimie had been crying out one second, and then nothing. Noiselessness. And that was somehow even worse than the screaming.

Now, a few steps from his open bedroom door, Madeleine stopped running. It was dark upstairs, dark outside, and dark inside Jaimie's room save for the glow of his computer screen. He had been watching that goddamn internet porn again. But that wasn't her concern, because there was something else brightening the blackness of her son's room.

Near the floor, in the darkness, eyes and teeth were aimed in her direction. Padmé's highlighter yellow eyes, her bared fangs, were facing Madeleine. Then the cat lowered her head, and Madeleine could barely see the charcoal Chartreux with only the shine of the computer screen to assist her. Though the sound that began to emerge from Padmé made what was happening clear to Madeleine, even before her eyes adjusted to the darkness.

It was the sound of an animal eating, the way only an eating animal can sound. Messy. Violent. Tearing and ripping and growling with effort.

Chewing.

"No!" Madeleine backtracked; her hand swept against the hallway wall until it found the light switch. She turned it on. Turned it off again nearly immediately after. But it was too late. What she saw in that brief burst of brightness would be burned inside her brain forever.

"Stop it!" The cat didn't stop. She didn't stop eating Jaimie's face. Didn't stop tearing at the strip of cheek Madeleine had seen being stretched from its bone when she had momentarily turned on the light. In that light, albeit fleetingly, she had seen Jaimie's cold, lifeless eyes. Had observed the pool of blood spreading beneath his head and neck, had seen the stillness of his body. She had witnessed the corpse of her only child being eaten by her fur baby.

"Padmé!" Madeleine prepared herself to charge the cat and spare her son's body any further degradation. But Padmé responded, stopping her in her tracks. It was the same sound the cat made whenever she was called by her name. A meowing. Sweetly.

"Padmé, *why?*" Madeleine cried again, now inching toward the cat, as if in hopes of negotiation. Padmé seemed open to communication as well; she turned her bright eyes to her owner and meowed once more.

But this time there was something strange about the meow. The meow, it echoed.

"Padmé?" Madeleine asked, confused.

Padmé let out a response, and Madeleine could see those teeth again. Her eyes had adjusted to the dark, making the cat and Jaimie more visible. Madeleine clearly saw the mouth lower, those fangs slide into her son's flesh as Padmé watched her. Yet the sound of meowing did not stop.

I must be losing my mind, Madeleine thought. She covered her ears with her hands and hoped the sound would cease. And it did. But when she removed her hands from her ears, she heard it again. Meowing. It wasn't in her head. The meowing – Padmé's specific meow, the sound that made Madeleine think the little creature special, one of the reasons she had brought her back from the dead – was coming from outside.

"Stop it, Padmé!" While Madeleine had been in doubt of her sanity, Padmé continued consuming Jaimie's cadaver, the cat's mouth in line with his eye. The noise she made was unsettlingly unspectacular. It sounded like it always did when Padmé ate wet food.

"*Please*, stop it!" Padmé continued to ignore her. Like most cats, she only listened when she felt like it.

There was the meowing again, again from some distance. Madeleine peeled her eyes away from the feast Padmé was making of her son. She ran to her bedroom, to the open window from which she could see the street in front of her house, from where the meowing sounds were emanating. The street where, two years ago, she had found her sweet cat's corpse. A finding that had led her to the madness now in front of her.

The street was typically poorly lit at night, something that had always riled Madeleine. But as she looked out of her window, she saw the world outside was nearly shining. The nature of the illumination confused and disoriented her. The horizon looked like a starlit sky.

There were spots of light everywhere; on the ground, along the treeline, across the road, all over the neighborhood. It seemed as though the constellations had fallen and had landed on the surface of the street.

But the cosmos hadn't come crashing to the concrete, Madeleine realized with a gasp, with a groan, with a sense of great foreboding. What she was looking at were eyes, dozens and dozens of eyes; Padmé's eyes, each pair. And they glowed at her in the gloom, a galaxy of glares.

They were moving. Slowly approaching.

"No!" Madeleine shouted out into the street. "Stay back!"

But they didn't.

The luminous orbs, they advanced, gradually inching their way onto her lawn, brightening the dark around them while darkening Madeleine's mind. She thought of her husband, who was likely dead at the facility. And of Dr. Gene and his staff. But she thought mostly of her son, in his room, his body now a meal. She imagined herself meeting that same fate, though worse a hundredfold. Her last thought, before fear overtook her mind and made no true thought possible, was of Barbra Streisand. She damned that wretched woman to oblivion for influencing all of this.

"Noooo!" Madeleine moaned as she watched the cats – the many copies of one cat – come closer. She knew, the way prey often instinctively knows, that they were watching her as they stalked slowly, crept toward their common goal, like the hunters they were.

From her neighbors' roofs, from the trees, from the road, from her lawn, they drew nearer. Their intent clearer.

Everywhere, in the darkness, she saw eyes, eyes, eyes.

And teeth.

The Cost and Consequences of Cloning Your Pet

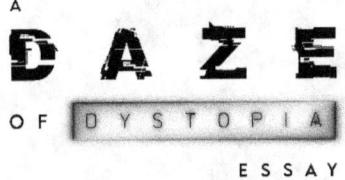

A
D A Z E
OF DYSTOPIA
ESSAY

BY FELIX I.D. DIMARO

I was surprised by two things when I first learned about the pet cloning industry. The first being that I, and nearly everyone I spoke to about it, had no clue that commercial pet cloning existed. The second thing I was surprised about was how much I seriously considered whether I would clone my poor sweet dead cat, Cat, if I were given the resources to do so.

My cat, Cat. There wasn't a bag she encountered that she didn't try to wear. She died late in 2022 after developing a massive tumour on her chest

In the past, I would not have given the hypothetical scenario of cloning my cat any thought. Death is a natural thing, suck it up and move on, is what my mindset would have been. Then I lost Cat due to cancer, and the idea of having another her seems incredibly appealing. Mourning tends to change the way a person looks at things. And that is the problem with the pet cloning industry, many of its naysayers say; the companies offering to duplicate your pet for exorbitant amounts of money are often accused of preying on people who are emotionally vulnerable. On the surface, the idea seems great. You can clone your pet, you never have to lose your little fur baby. Imagine: that perfect little cat or dog or hamster can be yours until you die. Mourning a pet can be a thing of the past. But can it truly? Can you really reproduce your pet? And what are the consequences of attempting to do so? This essay explores the cost and consequences of the pet cloning industry, both monetary and ethical. And whether that cost is worth the consequences it brings about.

THE FIRST OF THE CLONES

Dolly the sheep was huge news. I still remember, as a kid in 1996, how amazed I was by the idea of an animal being cloned. It was like something out of the movies, or the comic books I was obsessed with at the time. *Jurassic Park* had been out for three years, *Multiplicity,* starring Michael Keaton came out the same summer Dolly was cloned, and the *Spider Man Clone Saga* was going on as well (I LOVED Scarlet Spider). Cloning was such a fantastical thing to think of. Then I never gave it much more thought after that. Not in any practical, real-world sense other than the occasional rumours one would hear about science imitating art by bringing back extinct animals. Rumours I never put much stock into until recent years (more on that later). But as for something as seemingly improbable as being able to clone a household pet? I hadn't even considered it until I heard of Barbra Streisand and her dogs at the end of 2023. The legendary singer and filmmaker has been open about cloning her 14-year-old Coton du Tulear, Samantha, after she passed away. Streisand was able to have two genetic duplicates made, Miss Violet and Miss Scarlett. I was mind blown by that news, astonished that I hadn't heard anything about it after so many years. And after falling down a bit of a pet cloning internet rabbit hole, I was even more surprised to find that rich folk had been cloning their pets for over a decade prior to Barbra Streisand's cloning of Sammie in 2017.

Barbra Streisand with her two cloned dogs, Miss Violet and Miss Scarlett. Photo via Variety

The first cloned pet was born on December 21, 2001, in College Station, Texas. She was a calico named CC, short for Copy Cat (or Carbon Copy), made with the genetic material from a cat named Rainbow. It was done via reproductive cloning, a process that involves removing a mature somatic cell, such as a skin cell, from the animal to be cloned, and transferring the DNA into an egg cell that has had its own DNA-containing nucleus removed. The egg then develops into an early-stage embryo in a test-tube until it can be implanted into the womb of an adult female of the species. Science. CC was cloned by a team of scientists led by Dr. Duane Kraemer, a professor at Texas A&M University. Copy Cat produced three kittens of her own in 2006. And while many worried that cloned animals would live shorter lives than their non-cloned counterparts, CC lived until March of 2020.

Copy Cat in a beaker. Photo via Texas A&M University

Not long after Dolly, animals such as mice, cows, goats, pigs, rabbits, and cats were cloned, but cloning dogs proved to be more difficult than other mammals due to differences in their reproductive systems. it wasn't until 2005 that a dog was successfully cloned. A team of South Korean scientists were able to produce a pair of Afghan Hound puppies from the genetic material collected from the ear-skin of a dog named Tai. Only one of the dogs survived, the other succumbing to pneumonia not long after birth. The surviving dog was named Snuppy. And not only did Snuppy live for ten years (the average lifespan of an Afghan hound is eleven years), but his DNA was used to produce ten more clones in 2008, all of whom are said to have had normal lives.

Dolly the Sheep. Photo via The Roslin Institute, The University of Edinburgh

Both CC and Snuppy were breakthroughs, revolutions in science, and paved the way for commercial pet cloning. There are now pet cloning companies all over the world. And while prices vary, anyone with the means can typically clone a cat from between $25,000 to $100,000 USD. Dogs can be more expensive. According to the US based company, Viagen (www.viagenpets.com), their price for dog and cat cloning is the same: $50,000, paid in two equal installments. Their price for horse cloning, however, is $85,000, also paid in two equal installments.

THE COST OF CLONING PETS

I mentioned the price of cloning your pet above, but what I am concerned with here is the non-monetary cost of pet cloning. Most importantly, the cost to the non-cloned animals that are part of the process. Particularly dogs. Because not every clone pregnancy is successful, with many expiring in utero or dying shortly after birth, it takes several dogs to produce a clone. While the cloning procedure has improved since Snuppy entered the world, it took upwards of 1000 embryos implanted into 123 surrogate dogs for Snuppy and his twin to be born. This is essentially the harvesting of animals for the purposes of appeasing people who don't want to deal with mourning. For all animals involved in the cloning process, surrogates are needed, harmful surgeries and the toll of pregnancy must be endured, and many animals – both imperfect or unwanted clones, and surrogates who have no further use – are put to death routinely.

According to Vicki Katrinak, the animal research issues program manager of the Humane Society of the United States: "The Humane Society of the United States opposes cloning of any animals for commercial purposes due to major animal welfare concerns. Companies that offer to clone pets profit off of distraught pet lovers by falsely promising a replica of a beloved pet. With millions of deserving dogs and cats in need of a home, pet cloning is completely unnecessary." And, in an interview with NPR, Dr. Duane Kraemer, who cloned CC, said that people shouldn't clone their pets for sentimental reasons, stating: "We don't really need more cats. I encourage people to go to the pound and adopt a cat."

Snuppy (on the right) with his genetic father, Tai. Photo via Getty Images

THE POTENTIAL BENEFITS OF THE CLONING PROCESS

It all seems a bit like mad science, the idea of rich people cloning their dying pets because they can afford to circumvent the process of mourning. If that was all cloning was used for, I would think it would be rather pointless and self-serving. But there are legitimate scientific reasons to clone animals. Unique or rare animals, such as service dogs, can be cloned for research purposes or to make them more accessible to those who need them. Endangered species can be cloned for the sake of conservation. Researchers are also looking to combine cloning and genome editing to create animals that are resistant to certain diseases like bacterial infections and tuberculosis.

Cloning technology can also be applied to human medical innovation. According to the BBC, Scientists at the Oregon Health and Science University Center for Embryonic Cell and Gene Therapy have used some of the processes involved in Dolly the sheep's cloning to prevent the transmission of rare mitochondrial disease from human mother to child. The process involves transferring the nucleus of the mother's egg into the healthy egg of another woman while leaving the majority of the damaged mitochondria behind. This technique is referred to as a "three-person baby."

In Germany, which has one of the lowest organ donation rates in Europe, the Center for Innovative Medical Models has developed a plan to clone genetically identical pigs whose organs will be suitable for harvesting and transplanting into humans via a process called xenotransplantation (the transfer of living cells, tissue, and/or organs from non-human species into humans). This would assist over eight thousand people in Germany who are living with organ failure and have no treatment options. This process isn't without its detractors, many of whom state that pigs shouldn't be used in this way.

Far more controversial than the situation in Germany, scientists have cloned human embryos for the purpose of creating embryonic stem cells that, potentially, could help to cure many diseases including, but not limited to, diabetes, lymphoma, inherited immune disorders, bone marrow cancers, Alzheimer's, Parkinson's, spinal cord injuries and more. Possibly even more controversial than the above is the use of cloning technology to bring back extinct animals via a process called de-extinction, which is basically the plot to *Jurassic Park*. Michael Crichton (the author of the book that the movie franchise was adapted from) was prescient with the premise of his story. These animals would be brought back in order to return them to habitats they would still be present in had it not been for human interference. Many of these animals would greatly benefit the ecosystems they once thrived in. Currently, a few of the animals being pushed for de-extinction are the dodo bird, the woolly rhinoceros, the Pyrenean ibex, the Tasmanian tiger, and the woolly mammoth.

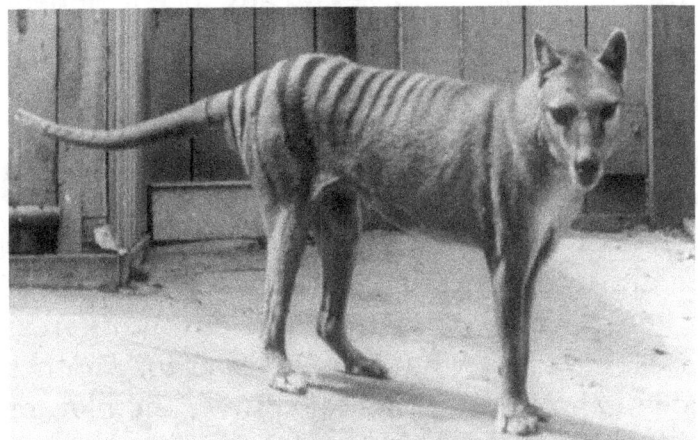

The Tasmanian tiger, thought to be extinct since 1936. There are claims that it still wanders the bush of Tasmania. (Image credit: Dave WATTS / Contributor via Getty Images)

THE HORROR OF IT ALL

The cloning of pets, if not unethical, is unnecessary. And, unless done so for positive reasons such as those stated above, it is a waste of resources that could be used to help humans and animals suffering around the world. But the same could be said about many industries. Such is the way of humanity. What I am interested in, as an author of horror and speculative fiction, is what the cloning of pets might lead to. Is it an inevitable step toward cloning humans?

According to the Center for Genetics and Society, only approximately 46 countries have formally banned human cloning. Less than a quarter of all countries. As mentioned above, human embryos have already been cloned. From my understanding of humans, if the technology is there, and the curiosity is there, whether or not it is ethical, we're going to do that thing. Do I think there will be human clones walking around out there in my lifetime? I wouldn't rule it out. It's one of the many uncomfortable scenarios I thought of when Barbra Streisand reignited my interest in cloning and what it might lead to. Another idea I thought up was, of course, the plot for this book, which I hope you found entertaining despite some of the liberties I have taken with the science behind cloning for the sake of the story.

SHOULD YOU CLONE YOUR PET?

I try not to tell people what they should and shouldn't do, but considering the harm done to so many animals in order to create a cloned pet, I personally am not for it. Aside from the harm done to animals, cloning a pet is a bit pointless. When you clone an animal in hopes of getting an exact duplicate of your beloved pet, you're going to be left disappointed. Cloning companies prey on the emotionality and bereavement of people with a lot of money.

These people often expect a carbon copy, but what they really get is a pet that is similar though not quite the same. In some cases, cloning won't even produce an identical looking pet. For example, CC, the first cloned cat, looked almost nothing like her genetic donor, Rainbow.

 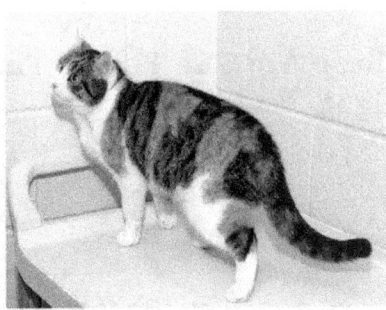

CC, the first cat ever cloned   Rainbow, the cat that donated the genetic material

Does CC look like a clone of Rainbow?

Image via Texas A&M University

Just because a pet carries the same genetic material doesn't mean that the genes will present themselves in the same way. Markings and eye colour can be different. What is a certainty is that you will not get a pet that has the same exact personality as the animal it was cloned from. As Barbra Streisand said, regarding her two cloned dogs, "You can clone the look of a dog, but you can't clone the soul." An animal's personality, similar to a human's, is dependent on its environment and experiences. A pet owner considering cloning their dead pet would be better off getting a natural animal of the same breed as the one they are mourning. It would save them some disappointment, it would save animals from going through unnecessary surgeries and pregnancies, it would save animals from being destroyed in shelters and laboratories. And, if none of that matters, it would save them roughly $50,000.

These Are The Things That Keep Me Up At Night

THANKS FOR READING!

You never know what might inspire you. I wouldn't have thought Barbra Streisand would have any influence over my writing. I don't know much about the legendary actress and songstress, other than she has been a legend since before I was born. And she inspired the 2010 banger of a club anthem, "Barbra Streisand" by Duck Sauce. Obviously her career has been very influential.

While it was no secret, I had no idea about pet cloning. Finding out about Barbra Streisand's two cloned dogs (while listening to *The Dan Le Batard Show with Stugotz* podcast, not while watching her interview on *Entertainment Tonight*) changed the way I look at pet ownership, human innovation, and what cloning might lead to.

You may have noticed that this novelette and the essay that followed it are both subtitled with the term *"Daze of Dystopia." Daze of Dystopia* is a two-pronged series I am launching with *In the Darkness, Eyes and Teeth*. In each book, I will write about a dystopian aspect of our modern world, both as a work of fiction and as a corresponding essay that goes a bit further into the details of what inspired the story, and the impact it might have on our society.

My intention is for my *Daze of Dystopia* series to result in a collection or few down the road. More details to come. In the meanwhile, you can follow me on Substack, and on Instagram @thingsthatkeepmeupatnight to stay updated on my *Daze of Dystopia* series and other future projects.

A few special thank yous: to Courtney Swank, for helping put together this and the rest of my books, and being very patient while doing so; to Ally Sztrimbely, for editing all my work, and fighting with me when necessary; to Rosco Nischler, for this beautiful cover and all the amazing artwork over the years; to my poor sweet dead cat, Cat, for existing, and sending me down this path of pet grief horror, resulting in some of the most fun I've had writing. And to my brother, Fred, who I dedicate everything I write to.

And thank YOU for reading this book, and all the other words of mine you've read thus far.

Dimaro
April 15, 2024

AVAILABLE NOW!

Viral Lives: A Ghost Story

Simon Hinch is a Gore Reporter. He spends late nights in bad places hoping to record violence for a fee. When Simon stumbles upon a man, bloody and dying in the street, he decides to film him instead of help. His footage is a viral sensation, and life is good for Simon. But it turns out that he may not only have captured a man's death on his phone, he may have captured a dead man's soul.

Want more cat related horror? Check out
Humane Sacrifice: The Story of the Aztec Killer

Losing a pet is never easy. For Melvin Cockburn – fortyish, alone, living in his mother's basement – losing his cat, Lucy, means losing his only friend.

When Lucy is diagnosed with cancer and given no chance to survive, Melvin is desperate for a solution that might save her. When all seems lost, he is approached by a peculiar stranger. Someone who claims to have an alternative method of treatment for his poor, dying cat. What Lucy needs to survive on is life. What she hungers for is a sacrifice or few. And all Melvin has to do to save his cat is provide her with a feast of human souls.

www.ingramcontent.com/pod-product-compliance
Lightning Source LLC
Chambersburg PA
CBHW051925220626
47052CB00003B/578